HOW TO GET RID OF A VAMPIRE

How to Get Rid of a Vampire

Using Ketchup, Garlic Cloves and a Bit of Imagination

J.M. ERRE

Translated by
SANDER BERG

Illustrated by
CLÉMENCE LALLEMAND

ALMA JUNIOR

ALMA BOOKS LTD
3 Castle Yard
Richmond
Surrey TW10 6TF
United Kingdom
www.almajunior.com

How to Get Rid of a Vampire first published in French by Rageot-
Éditeur in 2016
This translation first published by Alma Books Ltd in 2017
© Rageot-Éditeur, Paris, 2016
Translation © Sander Berg, 2017

Cover and inside illustrations: Clémence Lallemand

J.M. Erre and Sander Berg assert their moral right to be identified as the
author and translator respectively of this work in accordance with the
Copyright, Designs and Patents Act 1988

Printed and bound by CPI Group (UK) Ltd, Croydon, CR0 4YY

ISBN: 978-1-84688-422-1

FOR

Wednesday
1st January

Dear Diary,

Today something awful happened, something horrendous and horrific! It was even more awful than when my cuddly penguin lost its eye, more horrendous than the time they served us spinach in the canteen, and more **horrific** even than when I found out that Father Christmas doesn't ex... (Oh no, to this day I can't bring myself to spell it out, that's how horrendous I find it.) Anyway, something awful, horrendous and horrific happened today!

Before I continue, *dear diary*, I should introduce myself. This is the first time I'm writing on your pretty white pages and you haven't got a clue who I am. That's not very polite of me, and my parents keep telling me to be polite. (If you don't know what I mean by "parents", you're lucky!)

So there we are: my name is {ZAZIE}, I'm a girl, and when I think of the fact that, when I was born, there was a fifty-per-cent chance that I would have been a boy, it gives me the shivers. Are you a boy, dear diary? If you are, I feel sorry for you.

But let's come back to the main thing: ME, because dear diary, I have a feeling you can't wait to find out a bit more about me. OK, since you insist, here's a summary:

1. I am **VERY** pretty.
2. I am **VERY** intelligent.
3. I am **VERY** nice.

My flaws? I can't think of anything off the top of my head… Oh yes, I come with a manufacturing defect! My parents are to blame for that. They didn't finish their job properly when they made me. I lisp a little and have trouble properly pronouncing the S (I say "*th*oup" instead of "soup" for instance). However, I am perfectly fine with the Z. That's why *I love* my name: **ZAZIE**. (Just imagine if I'd been called Susie, that is to say "*Thuth*ie"!)

Your name, dear diary, is written on the cover: "Diary, 16 x 21 cm, premium-quality paper, made in China". I don't want to offend you, but that's not a great name. If you agree, I'll call you **Z**ebulon, because names beginning with a **Z** are the best! And, unfortunately for you, you're probably a boy (I'm *so* sorry for you).

And if you don't like your name, tough luck. You're MY diary!

Now that we have been properly introduced, I can reveal the awful, horrendous and **horrific** thing that I found out today. My cousin Lucas is coming to our house on Saturday! Horror of horrors! Why? Because this Saturday I had invited all my best friends to come and play with me. And now Mum has asked me to cancel it!

Do you know what a best friend is, dear diary? In your case, it's simple. Your best friend: that's me. Because I'm your ONLY friend. (Please don't cry, it's better than having none.) In my case,

anaïs

it's a little bit more complicated. I have two and a half best friends. Why "and a half"? Because Anaïs is my best friend every other day. The days in between we can't stand each other.

I have to say that Anaïs has a **VERY** bad temper, and she's a liar too. Of course, she'll tell you that *I'm* the one who has a bad temper. Whatever!

My other two best friends are called Julie and Kenza. We've known each other since nursery school. We've used each other's cuddly blankets and used to make it impossible for anyone to have a nap with our endless talking. Things like that create a bond.

I never argue with Julie and Kenza. They always do exactly what I tell them: they really are **VERY** good friends!

It would have been ideal to get together as friends on Saturday, just before the end of the holidays. And now everything has been ruined because I have to entertain my cousin Lucas! You can't imagine, dear **Z**ebulon, what a drag this is, because you don't know what he's like.

He's like a cross between Shrek, because of his looks, and Shrek's donkey, because of his intelligence. He has a head like a potato, and mashed potatoes for a brain! In short, he's a boy.

To give you an idea, this is more or less what he looks like (yes, I'm ALSO fabulous at drawing):

LUCAS

Anyway, ever since Mum told me he's coming, I've been upset, devastated, catastraumatized (I know that doesn't exist, but *I love* it)! It's not as if I haven't tried to talk my mum out of it: "Mummy dear, you can't just cancel my afternoon with my friends!"

"I'm sorry, but your aunt and uncle can't come on any other day. We'll invite your friends round some other time soon. Promise."

"Yeah, but Julie is moving house! I'll never see her again!"

"Julie is moving house in six months, and she'll be living less than two miles from here."

"Yeah, but Kenza is with her granny every weekend. She won't be able to come!"

"Kenza's grandparents live in Morocco. I'd be surprised if she visits them every weekend."

"Yeah, but Anaïs will probably be ill, because—"

"Haven't we told you not to say 'yeah, but' in this house?"

"But it's not wrong…"

"That's enough now, ZAZIE!"

I'd used up all my arguments, so I tried the last trick up my sleeve. I looked at her with my cocker-spaniel eyes, made my lips tremble and said with a choking voice: "PLEASE, Mummy dear!"

Apparently that works on Julie's mum. But mine knows no mercy. So I had to ring my friends and call it off.

Julie

"That's fine. My parents will be taking me to the cinema instead," was Kenza's reply.

"No worries. I've been invited to a party at my neighbour's house," Julie said, trying to comfort me.

"You're **SO** lucky. You'll have Lucas all to yourself," said Anaïs mockingly. (After that, we argued and fell out.)

Thanks a lot, friends! Thanks for sticking together! A good thing you're here, my dear **Z**ebulon. At least you listen to me and understand me. To show you how grateful I am I'll tell you something I haven't told anyone, neither my friends, because they are such chatterboxes, nor my parents, because they are my parents.

I'll let you in on a secret... my greatest secret!

Except that it's going to have to wait a little, because I've just heard my dad shout that he'll make me copy out lines if I don't come down in three, and he's already started to count (I wonder if he knows any numbers higher than three).

Maybe it's because Mum has called me five times already to tell me that dinner is ready?

(Someone needs to tell her that she sounds like a broken record.) Terrible things, parents. They always disturb you when you're in the middle of something. You can never be at ease in this house.

I'm sorry, you're going to have to be patient and wait until tomorrow to find out my secret.

Bye now, my **Z**ebulon!

Thursday
2nd January

My dear Zorro,

(I've changed my mind and decided to call you Zorro – Zebulon is ugly.)

Sorry again about yesterday. I had to leave you in a rush and join my parents for dinner. Not that it stopped me from being punished for something else, though. In the middle of the meal I had to sneeze with my mouth full. It wasn't my fault, but I can see where my parents are coming from. It's not great to have macaroni and ketchup sprayed all over your face. To make matters worse, when I saw their faces dripping in pasta and sauce I couldn't help laughing so hard I nearly choked! I think that's the thing they appreciated the least. Parents don't have a sense of humour, you know.

What's one more punishment, you'll say. It's true: I'm punished a lot. And all because of my imagination… I can't help it. I have so many ideas swirling round in my head and I don't always know how to put them in order.

My parents tell me I have **TOO MUCH** imagination. And that I talk **TOO MUCH**. And that I ask **TOO MANY** questions. Always **TOO MUCH** or **TOO MANY**. I can't help it they live life in the slow lane!

I'm glad, my *dear Zorro*, that you are there for
me, patiently listening to my troubles. It was
Auntie Bea who put you under the Christmas
tree, wrapped in beautiful red-and-gold paper.
I was a little disappointed when I opened my
present. Not that I have anything against
you, but I thought you were a box of
chocolates. And I really like, I
love, no, I *adore* chocolate! Not
to worry, though, I'm very happy
to have you. I plan to write in
you every day. I can feel I
already love you almost as
much as milk chocolate with
hazelnuts.

Dear *Zorro*, have you noticed anything strange
on your pretty white pages?

I made the silly mistake of leaving you open
on my desk while I went to look for some milk
chocolate with hazelnuts (I can't help it: if I talk
about chocolate I simply *have* to have some).

And when I came back I saw there were black paw prints all over you. Typical Roudoudou!

I'll explain. The one who shamelessly walked all over you was my tomcat Roudoudou.

I say "tomcat", but he could be a she. Roudoudou is so fat and hairy that no one has never been able to find out whether he is male or female. And goodness knows what you might find if you were ever courageous enough to explore his or her thick fur.

The last time I did, I found three Playmobil figures trapped in that furry jungle!

My friend Anaïs claims that Roudoudou is in fact not a cat at all, but some new species of animal invented in a lab by a crazy scientist. I actually think it's *Anaïs* who's been invented by a crazy scientist.

Roudoudou is softer and cosier than any blanket. If you put him on your lap to keep warm while you are watching telly, he starts to purr so loudly you have to turn up the volume. He has this in common with my granny: as soon as she sits down on the sofa, she starts snoring so loudly you have to crank it all the way up. And when you place Roudoudou on my granny's lap when she's on the sofa, just imagine the deafening noise they make!

When Roudoudou miaows, it scares our guests if they are not used to it.

The first time my friend Julie and Kenza came over to my house, they were shocked when they heard it.

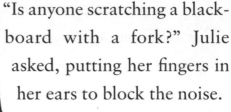

"Is anyone scratching a black-board with a fork?" Julie asked, putting her fingers in her ears to block the noise.

"Is someone watching a horror movie on the telly?" Kenza said, contorting her face.

"No, it's just my cat miaowing," I explained.

My friend nearly choked themselves laughing, telling me I had a wicked sense of humour. Then Roudoudou appeared in all his glory. It took them weeks to pluck up the courage to come and visit me again... So now you know who you're up against, my poor old *Zorro*!

Right, to make it up to you for having been so rudely trampled on by Roudoudou, I will keep the promise I made yesterday and tell you my greatest secret. Are you ready?

Here it comes: I have a secret hiding place underneath my bed. (I write this in small letters because it is a secret.)

I've had it for a week now and no one has noticed a thing, because it is an amazing hiding place. I'll tell you more about it…

Recently Mummy received a big book in the post. It came in a flat box. The cardboard was thick and felt soft to the touch. I knew immediately what I wanted to do with it. Straight after she had put it in the recycling bin, I announced that the bin was getting quite full and that I would take it to the recycling point because I am a VERY lovely girl who always helps her darling mother. That way I thought I might even get an extra reward.

Once outside, I picked out the cardboard box and put it under my coat. The rest I threw in the neighbour's wheelie bin, because the recycling point was too far to walk and I was in a hurry. After that, I snuck up to my room unnoticed.

In order not to be disturbed, I pushed my bedside table against the door. Then I got out my treasure and put it on the bed. It was a cardboard box big enough to hide a number of things in. I took a large roll of Sellotape and stuck it to the bottom of my bed.

It's the perfect hiding place… You can't see anything when you are making the bed or when you lift up the mattress or hoover underneath the bed. And no one ever turns over the base of your bed!

That is also where I've been hiding you, my dear *Zorro*, because my mother spends her days snooping around in my room as if it were her own! I think I'll also stick a sign on my door that says "No Entry". I have a right to some privacy, don't you agree?

So, what have I put into my hiding place apart from you? You ought to know, because you slept next to it last night. It's a book. A strange and wonderful book, both unbelievable and scary… Its title? **DRACULA**.

It's a novel by an Irish writer called Bram Stoker and it's about the most famous of all vampires: Count Dracula.

Do you know what vampires are, dear *Zorro*? They're terrifying creatures with some very strange habits.

Vampires aren't interested in sweets or chocolate. The only snack on their menu is human blood! That's what they live on. And they'll sink their fangs into your neck without so much as a by-your-leave!

That's what I learnt from **DRACULA**, a **VERY** well-researched book. People will tell you that vampires don't exist and that the book is just a novel, a made-up story. That's what everyone believes… But what if they're wrong? Vampires are diabolical creatures. They could have arranged things so everyone believes they don't exist. That would allow them to drink our blood in peace and quiet... Sure, people will say I have **TOO MUCH** imagination, but what if it were true?

Tell me, *my dear Zorro*, I haven't scared you, have I?

Sleep well all the same...

Friday
3rd January

My dear Zinédine,

(That's a bit more modern than Zorro, don't you think?)

As you have probably already guessed, the thing I like the most in the world is stories. Well, let's say I like them about as much as chocolate mousse. And chocolate eclairs. And chocolate truffles. And licking my fingers afterwards... Yum! Just thinking about it makes my mouth water.

Jeez, my dear **ZINÉDINE!** I've made the mistake of leaving you on my desk again to get a chocolate truffle (I couldn't resist). You're not angry, I hope? I promise you, this was the last time Roudoudou used you as his doormat!

So I was telling you how much I love stories. I'm lucky, because my dad is a **VERY** good storyteller (he needs to be good at *something*, otherwise he'd be *totally* useless). He's been reading stories to me ever since I was a little kid. Even when he's tired, even when he is in a hurry, all I have to do is look at him with my abandoned-kitten eyes for him to give in. Once you've figured which buttons to push on your dad, you can do with him as you please.

I also like reading on my own a lot. All it takes is a few sentences and I'm transported to a different world. I completely identify with the main characters. I laugh with them, I cry with them. I *am* them. Thanks to reading stories I've lead masses of lives.

I've been a medieval princess, a masked bandit fighting for justice, Tinkerbell, one of the Famous Five and even a perfectly behaved little girl (that's so me).

At home we have hundreds of books. My name is taken from one of my parents' favourite novels: *Zazie in the Metro* by Raymond Queneau. It's the story of a girl who talks non-stop and does exactly what she feels like. She's a right nuisance who messes all the adults around. Nothing like me, then. Ever since I was small I've looked at all those rows of books and wondered what is in them.

Just looking at their titles fills my head with ideas. I come across *The Count of Monte Cristo* and I imagine a great love story with princesses locked up in a crystal palace. I see *The Hound of the Baskervilles* and I become a courageous breeder of cute little kittens who has to fight off a mean dog who has decided to eat them all up. As for *Treasure Island*, that title was the cause of a big punishment I got for trying to cross the ocean in our bathtub. The whole bathroom was flooded. But it was hardly my fault. I was attacked by horrible pirates!

Last week I asked my dad if I could read **DRACULA**. The cover said it was a book about a vampire. The illustration showed a monster with big fangs, half-hidden behind a black cape and standing near a ruined castle. It looked dark, sinister and scary. What more could I ask for?

" **DRACULA**?" my dad said, pulling a face. "That's not for children your age!"

"Not for children your age." **ARGH**! I can't stand it when they tell me that I'm too young for something. So I told him: "You don't think I still enjoy Noddy, do you?"

"Noddy, yes, yes," my dad replied, nodding his head, thinking he was being funny.

"You know I'm top of the class in reading, right?"

"Yes, yes," my dad said, still nodding his silly head (he doesn't mind being utterly ridiculous).

"So when will I be allowed to read DRACULA then?"

"When you're old enough."

"When you're old enough" comes second on my list of expressions I can't stomach! It really *is* impossible to reason with parents. Do they still think I'm a baby or what? Too bad for them, they don't know who they're dealing with... Fortunately, the bookshelves in our house are spilling over, so no one's going to miss one book here or there. That's why, immediately after creating my secret hiding place, while my parents were busy in the kitchen, I took **DRACULA** from the shelf and hid it underneath my bed… Yes, that {**ZAZIE**} is a clever one!

For a week now, every evening, when the lights are out and my parents have kissed me goodnight to go and snore in front of the telly, I get my torch and open my **DRACULA**.

I make a cave with my duvet and three pillows, put my cuddly penguin next to me and begin to read… And to read **DRACULA** in the dark and silence of my room, I can tell you, that's proper scary!

I could tell you much more, but I've got to go and have a shower. Mum has asked me six times already.

My record is eight times. After that I wasn't allowed to watch telly for a whole weekend. I thought I was going to die. So did my parents

– that's how good I am at pretending to be dying. I'm a first-rate drooler – I should show you sometime. Oops, Mum has just called me for the seventh time.

I'll stop writing now because I am a reasonable girl and I don't feel like drooling tonight.

CIAO, ZINÉDINE!

actually . . . to make it as beautiful as I can. I am
beautiful, since I have the skill to use it
today. I just might to make my passage less bitter.
After all, you never know. It _is_ a chance
maybe . . .

My dear **Z**ebulon,

(It's kind of cute, after all, Zebulon.)

It's seven o'clock and I'm glad today is over. I had a horrendous Saturday. Do you remember ~~my idiot cousin~~ my cousin **LUCAS** who was supposed to come and visit? And yet I had something awesome planned for my friends. I actually wrote out the whole programme on a beautiful piece of paper and stuck it to the fridge last night to make my parents feel guilty.

After all, you never know, **LUCAS** might have a terrible accident and cancel his visit…

Your  darling daughter

Zazie's programme for this Saturday:

– Breakfast: croissants (big ones)

– Morning: watch TV and play on computer (in my PJs)

– Lunch: hamburgers and ice cream (lots)

– Afternoon: invite Anaïs, Julie and Kenza to a make-up session + play on 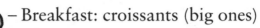 computer + have chocolate

– Dinner: pasta with ketchup and sausages (big ones)

– Evening (if I've been well behaved): watch TV in my PJs.

Obviously, nothing went as planned. First of all, I was very unlucky in that the weather was good. That's always a nightmare. Because when the weather is nice, my dad can only think of one thing: taking me out for a bike ride. And I hate bike rides! I bet you've never been on one, my dear Zebulon, so I'll explain how it works. Going for a ride involves leaving your house with a stupid-looking helmet on your head with the only aim to return hours later with sore legs. And you know what's really stupid? My dad loves it (no comment).

So after a breakfast of cereals and fruit (no comment), instead of spending the morning watching telly and playing computer games, we ended up getting sore legs while wearing a ridiculous helmet.

Then we ate fruit and vegetables (no comment) with Uncle Pierre, Auntie Bea and my cousin Lucas.

Oh that **LUCAS**! He replaced my girl friends in the afternoon programme. And I can tell you it wasn't easy to get him to take part in the planned make-up session! Even after I managed to tie him to a chair with my skipping rope, I had a hard time putting lipstick on him.

Seeing as he was moving his head in all directions, he ended up with lipstick not just on his lips, but on his cheeks, his forehead and his nose.

And because he kept on shouting "No, no!" I had to gag him before applying mascara.

There is only one thing **LUCAS** likes to do. Can you guess what it is? Going for bike rides! **ARGH**... Even when I proposed to play **DRACULA** we had to have an argument.

"I want to be the vampire!" he whimpered.

"No. You'll be the innocent young girl."

"But I'm a boy!"

"Yes, but you're wearing a white dress."

"Because you made me wear it!"

"And you have long hair."

"That's because you put a mop on my head!"

"And you're wearing lipstick."

"But you forced me!"

"That's what I mean, you're the perfect victim!"

All that I needed to do now was to sink my fangs into his neck and we'd be having a ball. But nope, he simply refused.

He's never up for any-thing, my cousin. He's just

useless. In the end I had to tie him up again so I could bite him... Playing with him is *so* tiring!

Oh, my dear **Z**ebulon, you have no idea how lucky you are to be tucked away all nice and snug in a box underneath my bed. No one comes to annoy you. No one forces you to do anything. All you need to do is enjoy the moments you have with me when I cover your pages with my pretty handwriting. And with grease, because I forgot to wash my hands after dinner. Sorry!

Fortunately I have Roudoudou. When Lucas had gone, I looked after him. I played with him, and cuddled and fed him. I felt a lot better after that.

Sometimes I ask myself whether Roudoudou is my pet or if I am *his* pet! A good thing I have you, my dear 💥... my dear Zoudoudou! That's what I'll call you from now on! Roudoudou and Zoudoudou, my two darlings who cheer me up when I feel down in the dumps!

How wonderful it is to be able to pour my heart out on your pages! I can get cross, criticize, walk all over you or cover you in tears, yet you never complain. Obviously you're only a diary. Still, good on you!

And fortunately I have my books as well! When your parents ignore you because they prefer to sit at the dining table for hours, listening to your uncle's funny jokes (not!). When your friends are far away because no one wanted to invite them. When your moron of a cousin refuses to play with you because he objects to being bitten, books are a girl's best friends.

Especially forbidden books, you know. Books you're too young for. Books you read in secret. They're the best! Anyway, I'll leave you alone because it's almost bedtime. It will be the best thing that's happened all day. I'll switch on my torch, build my cave, immerse myself in my book, and then DRACULA will come and get me...

Sunday
5th January

My dear Zoudoudou,

I'm sad today, because it's the last day of the holidays. Tomorrow I'll have to go back to school. I'll have to get up early again and sit still all day without being able to talk. It's *so* hard!

Dear Zoudoudou, do you know what a school is? It's a big building with classrooms where they teach you how to speak and write properly, and a playground where you learn swear words.

Fortunately I've got my friends. I have already told you about Julie, Kenza and Anaïs. I can't wait to see them again. In the playground we look out for each other, because it can be a VERY dangerous place on account of Kevin. He's a boy who spends his time running around, either after a ball like some little dog, or after his mate Sacha Chubby-Cheeks. So you have to be careful not to be in his way.

One day, our teacher Mrs Cuche, poor old Mrs Cuche, was unlucky enough to be in his way. She went flying and it was a beautiful effort for someone her age, except that her landing was somewhat lacking in elegance (a score of 3/10). I have to say, though, I don't know what possessed her to land on her teeth and cushion the fall with her nose…

Fortunately they make very good dentures these days, my mum told me.

The other danger of the playground are the spies. The worst ones are the twin sisters Charlotte and Camille Chalumeau. They have the same hair, dress the same and wind me up the same. Ever since nursery school we have been the best of enemies. All in all, I have two and a half best enemies. Because of Anaïs, every other day.

The Chalumeau twins look so alike that no one can tell Charlotte from Camille. To make things easier I always call them "Charmille". They hate that!

But sometimes, just to be nice to

Charmille

45

them, I call them "the spitting images" instead. That really drives them up the wall! I love it! Then they take the mickey out of my lisp. That's not ni*the* of them.

Wait, my parents are calling me... Aww shucks!... They've just had a great idea to spoil the end of my holidays: a bike ride! That's just what I needed! I need to find an excuse. Quiiick...

My parents are heartless brutes. I tried everything I could to escape their two-wheeled torture session. But no such luck.

"I'm sorry. I would have loved to come and make my legs hurt by cycling on little paths full of sharp stones, but unfortunately I have some maths homework I need to finish before tomorrow."

"Your teacher didn't set you any homework for the holidays. Get  your helmet and come."

"Yeah, but I twisted my ankle coming down the stairs just now and I—"

 "Zazie, we don't have stairs in our house. Take your water bottle and come."

"Yeah, but I've got to—"

"May we kindly remind Miss Zazie that the use of 'yeah, but' has been banned in the entire galaxy for all eternity. Take your bike and come."

"You're *so* mean!" I shouted in despair.

"You're *so* mean!" they echoed in unison, mocking me.

Parents are so cruel sometimes... I've just come back from a horrendous two-hour bike ride. I'm completely exhaustified (*I know that doesn't exist, but I love it*). And that's not all. Because on top of all that suffering I had the most bizarre experience… really frighteningly bizarre!

For starters, Dad got lost (that happens a lot), which added hours and hours to the trip. It was already getting dark when we passed in front of an old graveyard with a rusty fence. My calves were the size of watermelons and my parents were ten metres ahead of me. I was thinking about the best way to take my revenge on them when all of a sudden something appeared behind the fence.

It was a scary creature, half man, half beast, dressed in black, with a VERY pale face, a bright-red mouth and a hooked nose. When I caught his eyes – big, cruel eyes hidden beneath monstrous eyebrows – they flashed at me menacingly. It was horrible!

I was so terrified that my left foot missed the pedal and my hands slipped off the handlebars, and I landed flat out on the ground, lying there sprawled out like an old sock.

I wasn't hurt, but I hollered like mad, holding on to my knee. The aim was to get my dad to cycle home, fetch the car and get Mum and me out of there.

So I cried my heart out, accusing my parents of mistreating their helpless little daughter. Then I looked towards the graveyard once more. Night had fallen and the monster had vanished…

Had I been imagining things because I was so tired? I was just gearing up to cry more loudly (so they'd give me chocolate ice cream for dessert) when I saw something even more bizarre! At the exact same spot where only moments before I had seen the terrifying monster, something stirred. It was a black, hairy creature with wings. A revolting animal…

My eyes widened.
It was a bat.

I wanted to point it out to my mum, but it had already flown off.

My oudoudou, I'll leave you now. It's bedtime. *Officially* anyway… Because as soon as my parents shut the door, I'll open my favourite book and be alone with **DRAÇULA**.

```
22:00
```

Zoudoudou! It's getting late, but there is something I need to tell you. If not, I won't be able to sleep. I thought I would relax a little by reading my book. That didn't quite work out. When I picked up the novel, I stumbled upon a description of Count DRACULA. It was horrific!

To give you an idea, I'll copy out the passage:

His face was strong — very strong — aquiline, with high bridge of the thin nose and peculiarly arched nostrils; with lofty domed forehead, and hair growing scantily round the temples, but profusely elsewhere. His eyebrows were very massive, almost meeting over the nose, and with the bushy hair that seemed to curl in its own profusion. The mouth, so far as I could see it under the heavy moustache, was fixed and rather cruel-looking, with particularly sharp teeth; these protruded over the lips, whose remarkable ruddiness showed astonishing vitality in a man of his years. For the rest, his ears were pale and the tops were extremely pointed; the chin was broad and strong, and the cheeks firm though thin. The general effect was one of extraordinary pallor.

 I nearly fainted. That was exactly like the man I'd seen earlier today on the bike ride. A creature who hangs out in graveyards and transforms himself into a bat? Yes, Zoudoudou, I'm sure of it. I saw a *Vampire* today.

Whom can I share this secret with, apart from you? My parents? I know what they're like. They'll just tell me I have **TOO MUCH** imagination.

With my friends Julie and Kenza? They're such scaredy-cats they'll only be frightened. As for Anaïs, I just know she'll give me that look of "Sure, *we* believe you". That will  then annoy me, and we'll argue and fall out on our very first day back at school. I don't know what to do. I'll make something up at break tomorrow.

Tomorrow… It's strange, my Zoudoudou, but I have a bad feeling about this. I have a lump in my throat and my stomach is tied up in knots. It's not because I'm afraid to go back to school. It's just that I have a feeling that something bad is going to happen at school tomorrow.

Something truly **terrible**.

My dear ~~Zebulon Zorro Zinédine Zoudoudou~~,
diary,
(It's hard finding a good name for you, and it's
not like you're helping me by coming up with
suggestions!)

Do you remember the bad feeling I told you
about last night? Well, I was right, today something awful happened, something horrendous
and **horrific**!
   It was even more awful than when our
neighbour's drooling Dobermann tore the
head off my doll, more horrendous than the

time Kevin lifted my skirt in the playground, more horrific than the time Dad made me copy out fifty times: "I will come to the dining table when I am called. I will not talk back when I am told off. In fact, I must keep my mouth shut at all times."

The horror! The abominaciousness!

(I know that doesn't exist, but I love it.)

When I got to school this morning, I was in for a bit of a surprise when I heard that Mrs Cuche, our teacher, was not in. I like Mrs Cuche. Because she's a little deaf, we can chat in the back of the classroom without her noticing a thing. And because she can't see very well, in spite of her thick spectacles, I can give Charmille dirty looks without getting caught. In short, she's really nice. But why would she be absent? We knew she was coming up for retirement, because she had served her time and was all used up, but to leave before the end of the year? Whatever might have happened to her?

Everyone in the playground had their own little theory. My best enemies more than anyone else.

"We overheard the other teachers talking," Charmille started (they're always spying on people). "They said Mrs Cuche had broken her arm coming down the chimney dressed as Mother Christmas to amuse her grandchildren."

"I have an auntie who has a friend who knows the headmaster's brother," Anaïs butted in (she likes to make herself sound important). "She told me that Mrs Cuche had caught a terrible virus that made her lose her hair, teeth and ears."

It simply won't to do for everyone to have an opinion but not me, so I took on a mysterious air and whispered: "The truth is much more horrendous than that. An Irish friend of my parents', Bram Stoker, told me what actually happened to Mrs Cuche."

"So, what happened?" Anaïs wanted to know.

"He made me promise to keep it a SECRET," I said, putting on a disappointed face to make them more impatient.

"Aww, come on. Tell us! Please!" Charmille groaned.

"OK then, because it's you." (I love it when they beg me.)

When I'd gathered them around me, I whispered: "Mrs Cuche has been bitten by a vampire."

My revelation was a great success. The Charmille twin opened their mouths as wide as if they were about to  swallow a truckload of flies. And Anaïs's eyes nearly popped out of their sockets.

I was chuffed with the effect my explanation had. But just when I was going to laugh in their faces about how stupid and scared they looked, the bell rang and we had to line up to go to assembly. I thought I would take the mickey later at break. Little did I know that soon I would fail to see the funny side of it…

The headmaster stood up, wished us a happy new year and announced that Mrs Cuche had come down with the flu.

"The flu, my foot!" I whispered to Anaïs, showing her my canine teeth. Then the headmaster launched into some blah-blah which I didn't listen to, because Kenza was telling me how her dwarf rabbit had been drinking champagne on New Year's Eve. It sounded hilarious. Anyway, just before he finished his speech (finally!), he told us that our lessons would be covered by Mr **fleder**.

Then the headmaster moved aside and our new teacher stepped forward. It was a man dressed in black, like an undertaker. He had a **VERY** pale face, a bright-red mouth, a hooked nose and monstrous eyebrows. I thought I was going to faint. I knew this man… It was the man I'd seen behind the fence of the churchyard on my bike ride!

A scary creature who lurks around in graveyards at nightfall!

Mr **fleder** looked at each of us one by one with his piercing eyes. When our eyes met, I had the feeling that his gaze penetrated into the depths of my being. It sent shivers down my spine. My head almost disappeared between my shoulders and I felt a sharp pinch in my stomach.

 The lips of our substitute teacher opened. He gave a strange smile and said, "Let's go to our classroom." That's when I

saw them. In the corner of his mouth. His fangs…

(Mr Fleder has long, sharp canines.)

As for his name, "**fleder**" is the first half of *Fledermaus*, which is German for "bat"! You don't have to be Sherlock Holmes to figure out what is going on! Do you understand now, dear diary, what the awful, horrendous and **horrific** thing is I told you had happened?

Our substitute teacher is a *Vampire*!

We're at the mercy of a terrible monster who sees us as a huge supply of fresh blood. Some vile creature has worked his way into the school to prey on us.

And don't tell me that I have **TOO MUCH** imagination! Bram Stoker's novel is very clear about these things!

Tonight I'll plunge into my book again to study how Dr Van Helsing, the vampire hunter, goes about getting rid of **DRACULA**. I need to find out how to defend myself against a vampire. I need to find out how to stop one from attacking me.

I need to become *Zazie Van Helsing* , the vampire hunter!

Tuesday
7th January

My dear **Z**,

(I've decided to call you that, it's much simpler that way.)

I hope you're not too worried? You must be over the moon to hear that I survived my second day back at school.

I spent the whole day observing Mr Fleder. His fearsome appearance scared us all stiff. No one talked, and you could hear a pin drop.

Apart from that, he does his utmost to behave like a normal schoolteacher, which proves he is a VERY clever vampire. He made us work like slaves, and we did maths, geography, history, French and PE. We did more work in one day than we normally do with Mrs Cuche in a week!

When we had our break in the afternoon, everyone was tearing their hair out.

"My hand hurts from writing so much," Charmille 1 complained.

"My head hurts from thinking so much," Charmille 2 groaned.

"Let's pretend to our parents we're ill tomorrow," Charmille 1 added.

"If it continues like this, there is no need to pretend. We'll actually *be* ill," her spitting image whimpered.

I was rather chuffed to see my best enemies so unhappy. I was *that* close to thinking

Mr **Fleder** wasn't so bad after all… But I quickly focused on the **DANGER**. I'm sure Mr Fleder's aim is to work us into the ground. That way we won't have the energy to defend ourselves when he strikes.

A clever and sly vampire this one… Except that he hasn't met the real **ZAZIE** yet! To save my strength, I haven't done anything all day! Not a single thing. While the others were racking their brains over divisions, I pretended to be thinking deeply. Then, when we had to show our work to the teacher, I glanced at Anaïs's exercise book and – bingo! – quick as a flash, I copied down her answers.

67

I got everything right, and without having made the slightest effort!

And you should have seen me during our PE lesson. Not a drop of sweat. And that in spite of Mr **Fleder**'s cunning plan to turn us all into soft chunks of fudge, the easier to gobble us up: he made us run round and round the playground!

It goes without saying that Kevin was delighted. He looked at Mr Fleder as if he were God come down from Heaven.

You can be sure that when the vampire

strikes, Kevin will be his accomplice.

Meanwhile I had found the ideal hiding place: the girls' toilet. I squatted down behind the door and peeped through the keyhole. They were made to run for miles and miles until they were all exhausted. Halfway through the exercise, Sacha Chubby-Cheeks let himself fall, crying: "Help! Mum!"

And Anaïs was so red in the face she looked like an overripe strawberry (which I liked a lot). When Mr **Fleder** saw that the whole class was completely exhausted, he shouted: "One last round!"

"Already?" Kevin cried out, upset. Mr Fleder turned his head to look at him, and I used that moment to come out of the girls' toilets, as cool as a cucumber. I ran the last few metres pretending I was very tired. That was easy enough: all I had to do was imitate Charmille, who were dragging their trainers and panting like a couple of asthmatic poodles. Poor things…

Then, to finish us all off, Mr **Fleder** made us note down tons of homework in our exercise books.

It's obvious what his aim is. After a week of this regime all the pupils in my class will be turned into zombies, their brains all mushy and unable to resist him when he sticks a straw into our necks to suck up our blood as if he were sipping a cocktail.

I have very little time left to act. Right now, I don't want to tell anything to my friends, who will just attract the enemy's attention. Still, I could do with some advice. That is why I've just tried to talk about it to Mum while she was cooking dinner.

Since I had no clue how to go about addressing the matter of vampires, I started by talking about something else as a way of testing the ground.

"Cat food is strange," I said, scooping a few spoonfuls of the stuff into the dish of Roudoudou, who had just woken up from his third nap that afternoon.

"What's so strange about it?" Mum asked.

"Why do they make cat food tasting of chicken and salmon, but never of mice? That would really go down well with cats."

"Please, don't start with your absurd questions," Mum said, looking tired.

That was a bad sign. When she pulls that kind of face after my first question, it's not a good time to have a heart-to-heart.

 Just to be sure, I continued: "When I'm older, I'll make cat food that tastes of mice."

"When you're older you can do as you please. But right now, would you be so kind as to lay the table?"

I had my answer. Mum was not in the mood to listen to me. When you're faced with someone who does not see the obvious point of inventing cat food that tastes of mice, it's not worth bringing up the matter of your schoolteacher being a *Vampire*!

Is there really no one who can help me, then? Am I all alone in this? What if... *My dear Z.*, I've just had an idea. As I am writing on your pretty white pages, Roudoudou is asleep on my bed, curled up and purring away. What if I found a way of engaging him in the fight against the monster? What do you think? Yes, I know what you're trying to say. At first sight Roudoudou is not the most obvious of *Vampire* killers.

Seeing as it takes him twenty minutes to get from my room to the kitchen, taking three rest breaks on the way, picturing him taking part in a hunt requires a vivid imagination indeed. But who knows?

Perhaps behind his fluffy-cushion exterior (ideally suited to match a mega comfy sofa) a merciless killer cat is hiding, one who would do everything to protect his lovely and adorable mistress (me).

Let's not forget that in the past cats lived in the wild and had to defend their territory with their sharp fangs and pointy claws! They were probably a bit less

overweight than Roudoudou, for sure, but what if I put him on a diet? Oh no, that's

weird... As soon as I mentioned the word "diet", Roudoudou started to miaow! And he gave me a very funny look…

Nevertheless, cats are specialist mouse hunters. As I said, the German word for bat is "Fledermaus" and "Maus" is German for, well, "mouse". I'd seen Mr Fleder transform into one in the graveyard on the day of the bike ride. And that's when the monster is at its most vulnerable, small and powerless.

I must take Roudoudou with me to the graveyard this evening and…

What's this? Roudoudou has just started to miaow again. He does not look at all happy. Do you think it's because I mentioned taking him to a graveyard in the middle of the night? I think so. He's just started to scratch my pillow! OK then, I'll have to handle everything by myself.

Roudoudou really is **TOO** sensitive. He gets very irritable when you change his routine.

And now he's coming towards me, walking on the desk where I am writing… And he hasn't retracted his claws… I have a feeling he wants to play with you, my poor old **Z**. I'll have to tell him you had nothing to do with that diet idea!

The best thing is to stop writing right now and put you away (you know where) until things calm down a bit.

As for me, I'm going to bed. I need to sleep on this whole affair. But whatever I decide to do, one thing is for sure: I need to expose this vampire before anyone in the school becomes a victim (although if he really wants to, he can have Kevin). It's between you and me now, monster of the dark. I have no fear!

Well… maybe just a little…

Wednesday
8th January

My very dear Z.,

That's it, I'm ready for it. Tomorrow is the great day, the day I'll unmask the vampire! But just so you understand what I'm going on about, I'll begin at the beginning.

I needed time to prepare my plan, so I just **PRETENDED** to be ill. I am **VERY** good at play-acting, and my mum always falls for it. My technique is simple: just before my mother wakes me up to go to school, I rub my forehead very hard with my hand to make it feel hot. When she enters, I pretend to be asleep and

let out little groans. She then comes nearer and puts her hand on my forehead. She feels I have a temperature and wakes me up very gently, whispering in a worried voice: "Are you all right, ZAZIE?" (I love it.)

I LOVE iT!

Then I pretend to wake up, pulling a face as if I'm in a lot of pain. I act as if I have a headache or that my stomach hurts, or both, when it's very important like today. Mummy then goes to fetch a thermometer. After that, she leaves me alone to finish putting on her make-up and getting ready for work.

Meanwhile I stick the thermometer in Roudoudou's fur. He's like a hot-water bottle, my lovely big fat cat!

I need to be careful, though, because the temperature should not be over 38,5 degrees. If it's more than that, Mum will call the GP and stay at home all day and I won't be able to carry out my plan.

"You have a fever, my poor darling Zazie," my mother muttered, looking at the thermometer. "You can't go to school today."

"Oh no!" (I say this in a disappointed tone, as if to say "What a disaster! I love school!")

"Be reasonable, sweetie. You need to rest."

"Well, OK then. Aargh… (I say this in a despairing way, as if to say "Oh well, I'm dying anyway".)

"Do you want to have anything to drink, my sweetie-pie?" (Mothers get so adorable when you're not feeling well.)

"No, thanks… I don't think there's anything you can do for me… **ARGH**… (I need to be careful with my **ARGH**s so as not to scare Mummy too much.)

At this stage I need to put up with something unpleasant: take the fizzy and bitter medicine that leaves a taste like a bathroom air-freshener in your mouth. But I have no choice: if I want to succeed I need to be ready to do anything! So I just clench my teeth together (not too much, or the liquid won't pass) and drink the horrible mixture in one gulp, telling myself it's better than a suppository up my bottom, like when I was a baby.

The last thing Mum does is to ring our neighbour and ask her to look after me until noon.

OUR NEIGHBOUR

That's like winning the lottery! Because our neighbour is even older and deafer than our teacher Mrs Cuche! There are just a few awkward moments to get through when she gets here and gives me those prickly and wet kisses (she has hair sticking out of her chin and she dribbles a little, like I do when I pretend to be dying, although she doesn't do it on purpose). After that, I can rest easy. She won't move from the living room, where she'll watch soap operas with the volume on full blast. I'll have the rest of the house to myself!

The first thing I did as soon as my mum had left? I ran into the kitchen to scoff down a huge breakfast: a drink of hot chocolate with a big fat chocolate brioche, then toast with Nutella and an orange chocolate truffle to make sure I had a balanced diet (an orange is a fruit, and it's important to have at least five a day).

Then I went back to my bedroom and took out **DRACULA**. I made a list of all the main traits of a vampire:

1. They live on **Blood**.
2. They cannot stand garlic and crucifixes.
3. They have no reflection in the mirror.

I had made up my mind. In order to expose Mr **Fleder** I needed to do the **Blood** test. That's something vampires cannot resist. As soon as a vampire sees **Blood**, he goes mad. His eyes start bulging, he starts trembling all over and his mouth begins to water. Just like me when I see a chocolate mousse.

But how to get my hands on some **Blood**? To begin with, I thought of Kevin. He is always red in the face and spends his time running round the playground. His **Blood** is bound to be nice and fresh. I even thought that with a bit of luck Mr **Fleder** would like Kevin's **Blood** so much, he'd suck him dry, so we'd be rid of him once and for all.

But I had to stop fantasizing about this. Kevin runs all the time and I'm not fast enough to catch him. I also thought of my cousin **LUCAS**, who is easily tied to a chair. But unfortunately he lives too far way. The one time he could be of any use!

There was only one solution left. I had to make my own supply of **Blood**. First I thought I could use those juicy steaks Mummy had bought, and use Dad's orange press. If you can use an orange press to squeeze juice out of oranges, I thought, you could also use it to squeeze **Blood** out of a steak. Makes sense.

Well, you might be surprised to hear that it didn't work! And it wasn't for lack of trying...

I pressed the steak on the orange press for a while, but nothing happened. Except that the steak became all tangled up in the machine and that bits of meat went flying everywhere,

splattering the walls. Then the orange press started emitting smoke before it finally died. Apart from that, nothing happened.

The kitchen looked like a battlefield. Then I had a good idea. I went to the living room where our neighbour was watching telly with the volume at full blast. I explained that a nasty dog had entered the kitchen to attack our gentle Roudoudou, and that the place was a right mess. She was very nice, especially after I told her with my dying-person voice just how ill I was. She cleaned everything up.

Meanwhile, I had another great idea! I was not surprised, though, because I have them all the time. Since I was unable to get my hand on some real **Blood**, I was going to have to make some fake blood instead. The important thing was that it *looked* like **Blood**.

This is the recipe I came up with to make **Blood**. I took an empty jam jar and filled it with ketchup, Ribena, tomato sauce, grape juice, a splash of Tabasco and some water.

I stirred the mixture and added two ice cubes. It really looked like actual **Blood**. I had a taste, and then I drank it ALL up, because it was **SO** tasty.

I took my jam jar again, put some more ketchup in it, added a lot of Ribena, tomato sauce, grape juice, lots of Tabasco and a little bit of water.

I stirred the mixture, added two ice cubes and… I drank ALL of it again, because it was **SO**

Real Blood

tasty! Moral of the story: it's hard to make **Blood**.

After a few more attempts, I ended up with a whole jar of very real-looking blood. It's under my bed now. You'll be sleeping next to it. And tomorrow it will help me catch out the vampire! My only fear now is that I won't be able to resist the temptation to drink it all tonight…

During dinner, I couldn't think of anything else. I kept on playing the scene in my head in which I would expose Mr **Fleder**.

After a while my parents started to get worried. Normally I talk all the time when we're having dinner. So they thought my illness had got worse. Mummy even said:

"If you're not feeling better, you won't go to school tomorrow and I'll take you to see a doctor."

Not go to school? I would have jumped at the chance any other day! But my mission was to save the world from a terrible monster. I

couldn't miss school! So I
decided to launch into one
of my favourite topics:

"No, I assure you, I'm
feeling much better. I
was just thinking about
something. Can I talk to you
about it?"

Judging from their faces, they already regret-
ted not having made the best of the silence for
once, instead of encouraging me to talk. Too
late now, dear parents!

"Tell us, ZAZIE..." my mother said
hesitatingly.

"The thing is," I started, putting on my most
serious face, "that each year for my birthday
you invite other children round to come and
play, right?"

"Yes..." my father replied, sounding suspi-
cious, while my mother frowned, wondering
where this was going.

"So, why don't we ever invite round other cats when it's Roudoudou's birthday?"

My parents gave each other a worried look. My mum put her fork down as if she'd had suddenly lost her appetite.

"Well?" I insisted. "We could invite other cats round, couldn't we?"

"Don't you start again with your absurd questions," my dad said in an irritated tone.

"You'd better finish your pudding," added my mother.

I continued tucking into my chocolate pudding and smiled inwardly. Now they would leave me alone so I could work out my plan without being disturbed. I had won.

ZAZIE : 1
PARENTS: 0

Thursday
9th January

My **VERY** dear, adorable **Z**, whom I love,

(If you think I'm going too far, just let me know.)

Today was full of surprises, but I have to admit that it was a disaster. The **Blood** test didn't go so well. This in spite of my resisting to drink any of the fake **Blood** all through the night, on the way to school and waiting around in the playground. I was **PROUD** of my mental strength!

My plan was to leave the jar of **Blood** discretely on Mr **Fleder**'s desk and to see how he would react. I was sure he would throw himself on it and so show his true vampire face.

The problem was how to get close to his desk without being seen. Solution: use Kevin as a distraction. I'll explain: Kevin, who spends his time running round and round the playground, can't sit still in class.

All I needed to do was roll a little ball towards him. When it got to his feet, it all kicked off. Like a little puppy dog, **KEVIN** loves running after balls. When he saw the ball underneath his chair, he got very excited. He bent down to pick it up, but Enzo kicked it. **KEVIN** then crawled underneath Charmille's desk, who broke out in giggles. The teacher came up to them asking what the matter was, while Madjid picked up the ball and threw it to Jules, after which **KEVIN** jumped on Jules, who sent the ball flying across the room. Everyone was in stitches, our teacher was shouting and **KEVIN** was running round and round.

It was exactly the chaos I'd been hoping for, and it gave me the chance to get to the front of the classroom and put my jar of fake blood on Mr **Fleder**'s desk.

The problem was that when I got there **KEVIN** was just finishing his fifth lap around the classroom. I didn't see him coming and he ran straight into me. I let go of the jar and it flew through the air, spilling its bloody contents all over **KEVIN**'s head!

The teacher shouted VERY loudly. His eyes popped out of their sockets, he began to tremble and saliva was coming out of his mouth. There you had it. He had seen the blood and now he was going mad!

He opened the door of our classroom wide open and shouted that we should all leave at once, because he wanted to have a word with Kevin alone. Fortunately he hadn't seen that I was the one who'd brought in the jar of blood!

He was going to devour Kevin!

While my friends went to play in the playground, I ran to the headmaster's office. There was no one there. I asked one of the cleaners to come with me to our classroom to save Kevin. But she said she knew me and my antics all too well. UNBELIEVABLE! Me? Antics? She must have got me mixed up with Anaïs.

When I went to the playground to ask my friends for help, I saw the door of our classroom open and… out came Kevin. He was alive! How bizarre. How **VERY** bizarre. His hair was still covered in fake blood and his face was **VERY** white. As white as Mr **Fleder**'s. But stranger still was that Kevin was walking. Yes, you heard right, my dear **Z**! Kevin was neither running, nor racing, nor flying around, but walking as slowly as a tortoise. I'd never seen anything like it…

That is when I noticed he was scratching his neck as if a mosquito had bitten him, and I understood… Kevin had been bitten by a vampire who had sucked the blood out of him, draining his energy and turning him into a kind of zombie!

BIZARRE

I had read in my book that the victim of a vampire becomes one himself! So now Kevin was our teacher's accomplice! Where would this horror end?

As we were waiting in the playground for Mr **Fleder** to come and call us back in, I was completely stressed out. I saw the Charmille twins quietly talking to each other and looking in my direction, but my mind was too occupied elsewhere to take much notice. After a few minutes they approached me.

"Tell us, Zazie," Charmille 1 began. "Did you see who brought that red liquid into our class?"

Charmille

"What red liquid?" I asked, pretending to be mega-astonished, because I'm a great actress.

"The liquid that fell on Kevin's head," Charmille 2 made clear.

"I don't know. I didn't see anything."

"Is that so?" Charmille 1 smiled.

"Well, we saw the WHOLE thing," Charmille 2 added with an evil smile.

I felt a lump in my throat. I thought I mustn't let them see how worried I am. So I started to yawn as if I were utterly bored by their conversation. I should be in Hollywood!

"Really? So what did you see, then?"

Charmille had no time to respond. At that moment Mr **Fleder** called everyone back to our class. His tone made it clear that anyone who made him wait would be punished very severely.

My best enemies turned their back on me, sniggering to each other. I just stood there by myself with a lump still stuck in my throat.

What will become of me if the Charmille twins have seen me with the red liquid? What if they tell the teacher everything they know? At the same time, they can't prove anything… And like all of us they're scared of Mr **Fleder**. I'm sure they won't dare to approach him. Certainly not after the massive telling-off we've just had. He told us that if we ever created a ruckus again there would be hell to pay. And you know what, my dear **Z**? Everyone believed him.

Conclusion: the enemy is **TOO** strong for a *sweet and delicate* little girl like me. And finding someone to help me won't be easy. As usual, I can't count on my parents. This is what happened when my dad came back from work just now:

"*Dear darling Daddy*," (normally, that works really well to soften him up) "can I ask you something serious?"

"Something serious for a change? But of course, let's have it."

"You're not being very nice, Daddy," I said, whimpering a bit to make him feel bad. "You're always taking the mickey out of me!"

"I was just kidding, Zazie dear. It was an affectionate little joke." (Does he really find that funny?) "What did you want to know?"

"Do you believe in vampires?"

My dad raised his left eyebrow, while his right one pointed down. In short, Daddy dear looked like a fool.

"You call that a serious question?"

"I know no one believes in them, but just imagine they arranged it so that people don't believe in them."

"Can we not talk about something else?"

"What if they did it so they could hunt their prey without being disturbed?"

"What if we had dinner?"

"What if I'm right?"

"What if you were quiet for a change?"

"What if…"

"Shut up, Zazie!"

That was the answer Daddy not-at-all-dear gave to my serious question about the most important event since man walked on Mars (or was it the Moon?). Sometimes I wonder what parents are good for. What's the use of having children if you're always making them shut up! Am I right, or what, my dear Z… *My dear Zeddikins*!

I need to come up with a new plan now. In the novel **DRACULA**, Dr Van Helsing kills the vampire by driving a stake through its heart. I have to admit I am not really keen on using that method… To start with, I'm not great at DIY. The one and only time I tried to use a hammer to hit a nail, I hit a finger. It didn't hurt at all, because it was my dad's finger. But still. And then to drive a stake through someone's heart, that must be a messy affair. And I'm eager to keep my clothes clean!

There is only one solution: to tell my friends everything and turn them into my allies. I'll do it on Saturday evening, during a pyjama party over at Julie's. Kenza and Anaïs will be there too.

On the agenda: as many pancakes as we can eat, lots of giggles and gossip and, above all, coming up with a cunning plan to deal with Mr **Fleder**.

My own little Zeddikins,

(We're on very intimate terms, you and me.)

ARGH! It's horrible! I've been suffering from stomach cramps all day. I must admit that I overdid it a bit with the Nutella pancakes last night at Julie's pyjama party... You know what it's like: you have a laugh, you eat a pancake, you have a great time, you have another pancake, you bad-mouth the boys in your class, and soon you lose count of the pancakes you've had... Argh! I must have broken my record. I've promised myself I'll lay off

Nutella pancakes. At least until tomorrow.

Apart from that, I had prepared the climax of the evening well, which was the moment I revealed the true identity of Mr **Fleder** to my friends. You should have seen the faces of Anaïs, Julie and Kenza! A shame I wasn't able to take a photo!

Julie's and Kenza's jaws dropped. Anaïs's moody face, however, told me she was going to nit-pick and find something wrong. To convince them, I took out my secret weapon: *Dracula*, by Bram Stoker. I read the description of the vampiric Count, which sounded exactly like Mr **Fleder**. I pointed out the pale face, the blood-red lips, the monstrous eyebrows and, of course, the pointy fangs! Even Anaïs found it hard to swallow her saliva after that... Then I told them about the scary apparition of Mr **Fleder** at the graveyard the day I went for a bike ride.

I made much of the bat that had appeared at the exact same spot moments after the monster had disappeared, and I explained to them that the German for bat is "Fledermaus". When I was done I asked them what they thought of it all.

My two and a half best friends were in complete agreement: our teacher is a *Vampire*.

It was a solemn moment. We held each other's hands and swore to join forces in order to rid ourselves of this monster. Anaïs proposed we start a secret club.

Julie said she would design a logo for the club and make membership cards for us. Kenza announced she was going to design a costume, which her mother, who is a seamstress, would make for us.

I thought the most urgent matter, however, was to come up with a way to expose Mr *Fleder*. Still, I told Kenza I quite fancied a small red-and-black dress, a mask and pretty little lace gloves. In short, the whole thing was working out rather nicely. Unfortunately, then things turned sour... Guess whose fault that was?

When we said we needed a name for our club, Anaïs came up with "The Fang Extractors" (a ridiculous pun on "extractor fan" and "fang"), and Kenza with "The Garlic Crushers" (a very poor attempt at being funny), while Julie had no idea (so we avoided the worst). In the end I said they were lucky I was there, because I had a great name: "The Van Helsing Girls", a

reference to Dr Van Helsing, the vampire hunter in Bram Stoker's book.

That's when Anaïs put her oar in. And I mean all the way.

"It's not up to you to decide the name, ZAZIE," she burst out. "The most important thing our group needs to do is elect a LEADER, and it's the LEADER who will decide what we will be called."

"Who is going to be our LEADER, then?" Julie wanted to know.

"I think it should be me," Anaïs announced.

Her? LEADER? How dare she! My blood was beginning to boil.

"I was the one who discovered Mr Fleder's true identity," I said.

"But I was the one who suggested we should start a secret club," Anaïs replied.

"It's always the same with you! You're such a big so-and-so!"

At that moment Anaïs pointed at me and said with a snigger: "You call *me* big? Just look at yourself! You should lay off the chocolate for a while."

I nearly exploded. One more word and I would make Anaïs disappear from ~~Julie's bedroom the town~~ the face of the earth.

"Say that again!"

"I'm sorry," she said, pretending to look like she really *was* sorry. "I shouldn't have said you were big."

"That's better," I replied, feeling my calm return.

But then a mischievous twinkle appeared in Anaïs's eye and she contorted her lips into a horrible smile: "When I *th*aid you were 'big', I actually meant to *th*ay '*th*uper fat'!"

I felt something raging inside of me. Something violent, something terrible, something outragilious *(I know that doesn't exist, but I love it)*. Anaïs had committed the ultimate crime: she had mocked my lisp!

My beautiful skin turned bright red. My blood was positively seething and cooking my brains. I believe there was even smoke coming out of my ears! Julie and Kenza got scared and walked away from me as if I were a gas canister about to explode. Even Anaïs wiped her intolerable smirk off her face! Fortunately for her, at that moment Julie's mother came into the room.

It was time to go to bed. Anaïs had escaped by the skin of her teeth (which are much less pretty than mine). For the time being at least…

The outcome of the pyjama party: there will only be **THREE** *Van Helsing Girls*.

And I have a new best enemy. Once again…

Oh my poor **Z**eddikins, I believe that you have a best enemy too. Roudoudou has sharpened his claws on your pretty white paper! It's shocking, but I have the impression that my cat doesn't like you. Maybe he thinks we spend **TOO MUCH** time together? He must be jealous!

I should never have mentioned his diet to you. It must have rubbed him up the wrong way.

Monday
13th January

My dearest darling Zeddikins,

Today Julie, Kenza and I got together under the lime tree in the playground in order to hammer out the details of our anti-*Vampire* operation. The Charmille twins were busy "making themselves beautiful" in the girls' toilet. Given the size of their task, we could be at ease for a moment. As for Anaïs, she spent a while walking around us in circles without daring to come nearer, consumed by jealousy and anger. Serves her right!

Although Kevin had started to run round and round again in order to appear normal, I

warned my mates: "You can't trust Kevin. I'm sure he has become the teacher's accomplice."

"You're right," Kenza agreed.

"We never trusted Kevin anyway," Julie added.

"You're right," said Kenza, who always agrees with everyone.

"We must also be careful of Anaïs," I continued. "She is probably planning her revenge."

"Do you think she might warn our new teacher?" Julie asked, worried.

"I think she is capable of anything."

"You're—"

"I'm right, yes, I know, Kenza."

After that, Julie wanted to show us the logo she had created for our club, and Kenza got out her design of our costumes.

I told them we had very little time and that they had to listen to my plan first. But because I'm such a nice person I allowed Kenza to show me her drawing of my black-and-red outfit first. I'm going to look **SO** pretty in it!

My plan is straightforward. I will force Mr **Fleder** to reveal himself. I'll prove he's a vampire with the help of some garlic, a crucifix

and a mirror. Kenza will be on standby to help me. If the teacher attacks me, she'll place herself in between him and me to allow me to escape.

"Isn't it a bit **DANGEROUS**?" Kenza wondered anxiously.

"No, of course not," I said to put her mind at ease.

And I didn't even lie, because it was not a bit, but in fact VERY dangerous.

Julie too had a mega-important mission. As soon as the vampire began to writhe in pain faced with my weapons, we needed her to run for help so he could be captured. Kenza wanted to know if she couldn't swap with Julie. So I had to remind her we needed someone who was a fast runner and that she had come last in the cross-country race.

We went through the whole plan, step by step. After that we took the time once again to admire Kenza's design of my black-and-red outfit. I'm going to look so ♥*pretty*♥ in it!

112

My dear Zeddikins, in a few hours I'll know if my plan to capture the vampire will have worked. Tonight, as I'm lying in bed, I have to admit that my tummy hurts, although I've hardly had any chocolate all day.

I have prepared my weapons for tomorrow. I put crushed garlic in my school bag, as well as a small crucifix I found among my granny's things up in the attic, a mirror my mum uses to pluck her eyebrows and a piece of rope to tie the vampire up. I'm well prepared. Mr **Fleder** had better watch out!

There is only one thing left to do before getting some sleep to gather my strength. I need to write a few words to my parents on your pretty white pages.

Dear Mum and Dad,

If you're reading this, it means you have found my diary hidden underneath my bed (it's not very nice to be going through someone else's things, but I forgive you).

If you're reading this, my room will be empty, and my cuddly penguin, my dolls and my big old Roudoudou will all be in tears (because they loved me very much).

If you're reading this, it means that your darling daughter has gone to Heaven (because with all my great qualities I know I will be accepted straight away).

You need to know, dear parents, that I think of you up here on my little cloud. Even if you were mean to me and always treated me like a little kid and forced me to borrow chocolate from the kitchen cupboard because you didn't give me enough. And even if you were annoying, irritating, exasperating, tiresome and unbearable, I still love you more than anyone else in the world.

To wrap thing up, I want you to take care of my belongings. This is my last will and testament.

✿ To Julie I leave my Nintendo 3DS, including all my cool games. I hope she will play on it often thinking of me, as long as she doesn't break my records. A little bit of respect, please.

✿ To Kenza I leave my MP3 player with all my favourite songs on it. I hope she will listen to them thinking of me, as long as she avoids singing along to them all out of tune with her shrill voice. A little bit of respect, please.

✿☠ To Anaïs I leave my fashionable dresses. I hope she will wear them thinking of me, as long as she doesn't wear them together with one of her horrendous hairbands. A little bit of respect, please.

☠ To Charlotte and Camille (the Charmille twins) I leave… absolutely NOTHING! (Just imagine!)

☠ To Lucas I leave my awful pink bicycle and my grotesque Barbie helmet. He can do with them as he sees fit. He can have them for dinner if that is what he wants. I don't give a hoot: I hate cycling.

✿ To my beloved Roudoudou I leave all my cuddly toys he never had the right to get close to. He can chew on them or rip them apart with his claws or do whatever he likes with them thinking of me.

Signed: your darling little daughter {ZAZIE}, whom you already miss terribly.

PS 1: If you make a new baby to replace me, please don't make a boy, I beg you.

PS 2: If by any chance you do end up with a boy, I forbid you to give him my cuddly penguin.

Tuesday
14th January

My dearest darling Zeddikins,

I have good news 😊 and bad news 😟.
The good news is that I'm still alive (I'm sure
you figured that one out by yourself since I'm
writing in you). The bad news is that I wasn't
able to carry out my plan.

You're not going to believe it, but today we
had no lessons. Mr **Fleder** was off sick! That
takes the biscuit! Since when do teachers who
replace teachers who are off sick have the right
to be off sick themselves? Well, "off sick" in
quotation marks...

At least, that was the official version, but who knows what kind of diabolical truth lies behind this. Did he drink **TOO MUCH** blood and does he have indigestion (like the day I ate an entire Christmas pudding)?

Anyway, there was no substitute for the substitute and we were looked after all day by a **TA** from the nursery school, who said we could do any activity we wanted as long as it was a quiet one.

"Is talking a quiet activity?" Kevin asked the **TA**, who responded with a gentle "no", because she didn't know Kevin yet.

"Is running around a quiet activity?" Kevin continued.

"Running around in class? Are you trying to be funny?" said the **TA** with a big smile, because she still didn't know whom she was dealing with.

"Is making jokes a quiet activity?" said Sacha Chubby-Cheeks, while Kevin tried to work out what the **TA** meant, scratching his head and sticking a finger up his nose.

"Be quiet, please!" shouted the **TA**, who had lost her smile now that the class was getting rowdy.

"I don't get it," Kevin insisted. "Is speaking a quiet activity?"

"That's enough!" said the **TA**, irritated. Her cheeks had turned bright red. "You're in detention!" (Finally, she realized whom she was dealing with.)

I spent the whole day quietly writing down everything that has happened since the arrival of Mr **Fleder**. It was like a huge essay and

it contained lots of verbs, subjects, direct and indirect objects, adjectives, commas and full stops: the works!

I painted a portrait of the vampire and told the adventure in great detail. It was a huge undertaking! I needed two drafts, and the neat version consisted of ten pages. I also produced a drawing in black and red felt-tip of Mr **Fleder** dressed as a vampire, with blood dripping from his pointy fangs. It was a masterpiece!

I liked writing the story so much that I didn't notice the time pass. Even during break I continued scribbling in a corner. Julie and Kenza got worried.

"Are you **ILL**?" Kenza asked.

"No, I'm working on something."

"That's what we're saying: you're ILL," Julie insisted.

"Leave me alone and focus on your task ahead in our fight against you-know-who. It's only been put off until tomorrow."

"Now that you mention it," Kenza whispered, looking a little anxious, "are you sure that it's not a little bit—"

"No, Kenza. Let me say it once again: it's not *a little bit* DANGEROUS ."

Even the Charmille twins were a little alarmed to see me sitting in my corner writing. I caught them signalling to Anaïs that I was *Charmille* crazy (crazier than usual at any rate). I don't think I ever worked so much in my life! And I loved it!

I put the account of my adventures in a red envelope on which I wrote: "To be opened in case of tragic disappear-

ance." That way, if I get bitten by the vampire, the whole world will know just how coura-geous I was.

All the pupils will cry their eyes out (even Anaïs, I'm sure). And everyone will have to write an essay about a good memory they have of me (even the Charmille twins will have to write one, which is going to be very hard for them!). The headmaster will hold a speech in

my memory and talk about all my excellent qualities and about how irreplace-able I am.

Maybe they'll even name the school after me? That would be cool! If possible,

I'd rather avoid having a vampire breathing down my neck... But I would *love* for the school to be named after me!

My dear  (Zeddikins sounds a bit childish, no?), I can't wait for it to be tomorrow. It's not that I really want to see Mr **fleder** again, but there is nothing more annoying than having to wait. To make matters worse, Roudoudou has refused my caresses. I would have felt so much better had I been able to cuddle up to that big ball of fur. But I think he's got it in for me ever since I mentioned his diet... I must find a way of getting him to forgive me.

As soon as I'm done with our teacher, I'll get serious about that business of developing cat food that tastes of mice!

All I need to do now is try and get some sleep, avoiding any nightmares if possible... I hope our teacher will be back tomorrow morning.

Tomorrow's schedule: spelling test, maths, history and...

Z,

(I'm not very affectionate tonight, these are serious times.)

Horrible news: my plan has failed! Tonight, I feel totally demoralized. I don't even know if I have the strength to tell you everything. You really want to know? Are you sure? OK then, but only because it's you.

To expose Mr *Fleder* I decided to use the most efficient weapon there is: garlic. It is well known that vampires are allergic to garlic.

It's a bit like my uncle, who gets covered in rashes as soon as he comes into contact with Roudoudou's hair, with peanuts or with me.

When a *Vampire* smells garlic, he doesn't get a rash, because that wouldn't look very nice on his pale skin. Instead he starts hissing like an angry cat and disappears as quickly as he can without even finishing his glass of fresh blood.

I had decided on the ideal place for my garlic attack: the school canteen.

That's another thing I haven't mentioned to you before, my dear ⚡. A school canteen is a big and very noisy space that smells of chips, where you eat soggy pasta and over-boiled, stringy vegetables while trying to avoid a hailstorm of breadcrumbs thrown by the boys.

Apparently it's meant to relax us in between lessons...

My plan was to drop a few crushed garlic cloves into Mr **Fleder**'s food. With a bit of luck the mere smell would make him flee the school there and then. With even more luck, one taste of his garlicky shepherd's pie would make him writhe in agony on the floor. After that, he would be bombarded by breadcrumbs thrown at him by crazed pupils and he'd disappear for good! But first I needed to get near his plate...

I managed to get behind him in the queue at the counter. Julie and Kenza stayed close to offer support should I need it.

Even though I'm exceptionally courageous, my stomach was tied in knots.

As Mr **Fleder** and I were moving along the counter, tray against tray, my forehead was covered in beads of sweat. The vampire was standing right next to me. He looked huge, with his hooked nose and terrifying gaze. At one point he offered me a cruel smile, showing his pointy teeth. It was obvious he'd rather have me on his plate than shepherd's pie! In spite of that, I managed to keep my calm. When we got to the end of the counter, he started flirting with the chef in order to turn her into his next victim for a **Blood** donation. I leant over his tray to grab some bread and dropped a handful of garlic into his plate. That's what I call sheer talent!

130

Seeing as the first part of the operation had been a success, I went to sit down and enjoy the spectacle. Julie and Kenza joined me, both very excited. Our three pairs of eyes were fixed on the teacher, waiting to see him being unmasked as a vampire. But the monster's reaction was not what we expected...

Instead of beginning to screech like an enraged bat, he devoured his shepherd's pie in a few minutes, licking his lips! Worse than that, he cleaned his plate with a crust of bread, soaking up the last bits, and then got up to get seconds!

A MUTANT vampire, that's what we were dealing with! A new species of vampire immune to garlic!

I had put my faith in Bram Stoker's *Dracula*, but that book was written more than one hundred years ago. Vampires must have evolved since then, like everyone else. Time to write a new version! If not, how are we, the new generation of vampire hunters, to know how to go about our business?

Even though the garlic had failed to work, I was not going to give up so easily. I was determined to move on to plan B: the crucifix, the little cross with Jesus on it that burns vampires at the slightest touch.

Mr **Fleder** could not be immune against everything! I would pull out granny's crucifix like cowboys draw their guns in Westerns, and stick it under his nose. I'd then play the innocent girl and ask him: "Sir, I found this on the floor. Is it yours, by any chance?"

Except that, once again, it didn't pan out the way I had in mind... All that, *my dear Z*, because of someone you are getting to know very well, that most treacherous, most evil, most repugnant of all girls ~~of the school of this city~~ of the world: **Anaïs** .

As I was getting up to face the monster, I saw that **Anaïs** too had left her seat at the other end of the canteen. She gave me a sly little look and I knew she was up to something. But it wasn't until I saw what she had in her hand that I understood what it was…

She was holding a mirror! And not just any mirror: **MY** mirror, which she must have stolen from **MY** bag! It was the mirror I was going to use to pluck Mr **Fleder**'s teeth out. My last resort to unmask our teacher as a vampire, because vampires don't have a reflection (that way they don't have to see their ugly faces). That back-stabbing Anaïs had stolen my idea!

While Mr **Fleder** was quietly finishing his second plate of shepherd's pie, **Anaïs** started to run towards him to be the first one there. So I decided to speed up as well.

Each of us wanted to beat the other one in the final sprint, but we were headed for disaster… All of a sudden, Anaïs caught her foot on the leg of a chair, and I slipped on a slice of salami. I let go of the crucifix, and the mirror flew into the air, sparkling in the fluorescent light. And we crashed into each other at full speed, right in front of Mr **Fleder**.

It was a disaster. Not only was our teacher a mutant vampire, but the only ones capable of destroying him were lying on the floor, pretty much knocked out. The mirror ended its flight in the mashed potatoes of Sacha Chubby-Cheeks. Needless to say the pupils went wild. I even thought I saw Kevin dangling from the ceiling, but that must have been a hallucination due to the blow to my head.

That's when I had the most embarrassing experience of my entire life. Mr *Fleder* told Anaïs and me off in front of the whole school.

The pupils had left their trays and formed a circle around us. They were milling about, laughing. Breadcrumbs were flying left, right and centre. I even saw my best enemies, the Charmille twins, clapping their hands with a big smile on their lips… To be humiliated in front of the Spitting Images!

The teacher was even scarier than usual, his mouth twisting and showing his fangs.

"Zazie! Anaïs! What on earth do you think you are doing? Your behaviour is unacceptable!" (As far as Anaïs was concerned, I agreed.)

"I'm sorry," Anaïs the traitor said. "It was Zazie who—"

"I don't want to hear it!" (I totally agree with Mr **Fleder** there.) "You'll both be punished!" (Errm… I don't really agree with that…)

Just when I thought the worst was over, something else happened. The final blow was still to come. And it was delivered by Charmille, who stabbed me in the back by saying: "Poor Zazie! She is so clumsy! Ever since she dropped her jar of red liquid on Kevin's head."

When they'd finished their sentence, everyone stopped laughing because Mr **Fleder** looked like he was about to explode. Even his usually pale skin had gone all red!

"I'll give you a letter requesting a meeting with your **PARENTS**!" he shouted. (I don't agree in the slightest there.)

My **PARENTS**? I had to swallow hard when I thought of myself being convicted by a jury consisting of my parents. I wouldn't be allowed to play on my Nintendo for a whole month and be forced to go on bike rides every weekend… It would be horrid…

And then it all became clear to me. I understood the *Vampire*'s plan. Mr **Fleder** is not only clever, he's also greedy. He's not interested in us, his pupils. A child is **TOO** small and doesn't contain a lot of blood.

No, his aim from the start has been to get to our **PARENTS**! What he wants is to devour my mum! And that is **OUT OF THE QUESTION!** She never listens to me, she punishes me all the time, she gets on my nerves round the clock, but ~~I got used to her she can be useful~~ *I love my mum*.

I need to come up with a new plan fast.

I won't let that vampire get to my mum. As for my dad, that's open to negotiation. Maybe if he stops making me go on bike rides.

Thursday
16th January

My dearest Z, who is going to have to comfort his poor little {**ZAZIE**},

I'll tell you about the worst day of my whole life. So far, at least, because I'm afraid that tomorrow is going to be even more *horrific*...

After yesterday's disaster and Mr *Fleder*'s request to meet my parents, there was only one thing I could do: never return to school. When Mum came to wake me up I tried the good old trick of pretending to have a bad tummy so I could stay at home. All I needed to do was stick the thermometer in Roudoudou's

fur for a while for the
trick to work. But
I hadn't counted on
my parents' infinite treachery.

"Look what I bought, Zazie!" Mum told me,
looking very happy and waving a funny old
object in the air.

"What's that?"

"An electronic thermometer. You stick the tip
in your ear, you push the button and it gives
you the right temperature straight away. Look,
I'll show you."

I had no time to come up with an excuse, and
my mother stuck the torture instrument in my
ear! And then they say that new technology is
there to improve our lives!

"**NO FEVER!**" Mum said, excited. "I'll
give you a tablet for your tummy and then you
can go to school."

At breakfast I didn't know what to do. I
was really torn. Should I show them the letter

which Mr **fleder** wrote to tell them he wants to see them and which they need to sign? Sending them to see Mr **fleder** would be sending them straight into his waiting fangs. But if I told them the truth about my teacher, they would laugh in my face, like they always do! So I preferred not to say anything.

My goal for the day was not to be noticed by anyone and make everyone forget I exist. But, as expected, as soon as I walked into the playground, my teacher signalled me to follow him. Anaïs was already there showing him her letter… signed by her parents! The traitor!

"What about you, Zazie?" Mr **fleder** asked in an icy voice. "Can I see your signed letter, please?"

141

"What could I say to that? Tell him Roudoudou had torn it to shreds with his sharp claws? That I'd dropped it in the toilet, entirely by accident?"

I didn't feel I had the strength to lie to a vampire, so I allowed myself to get as red as a beetroot (as red as two or three beetroots even – that's how red in the face I was).

Mr **Fleder** must be able to read colours, because he

142

ordered me to show him the letter signed by my parents tomorrow, without fail.

The day at school was never-ending. All the pupils noticed I was feeling a little down in the dumps, even Anaïs. When she apologized for having stolen my mirror, I replied that it was OK and that I was very fond of her. My *kindness* so worried her that she went straight to Julie and Kenza to ask them if I was planning some terrible revenge (the answer is **YES**).

When the school bell rang at the end of the afternoon, I only had one thing on my mind: to disappear **VERY** quickly, get back home, lock myself in my room, snuggle up to Roudoudou and never to set foot in school again. But as the pupils were filing out of the classroom, I heard a voice behind me.

"Zazie, can I see you for a minute?"

It was Mr **Fleder**. I felt like my legs had turned to jelly, and my tongue was all spongy.

"ZAZIE" I whispered to Julie to wait for me at the door and keep an eye on us. Then I went up to him, walking very slowly.

The vampire was marking exercise books with a blood-red pen. He looked up.

"Julie, would you mind shutting the door?" he said sharply. "Thank you." Julie threw me a desperate glance, but I signalled to her that it was OK. I tried to swallow, but there was a lump in my throat. I was his captive. The end was near...

At that moment, as if he were getting ready to pounce on me, he hunched over his desk. Then, to prolong my torture, he opened a drawer. What was he looking for? A straw to drink my blood with?

"I would like to know if you were the one who wrote this," he said, straightening himself.

In his hand he held a red envelope. I knew immediately what it

to be opened in case of tragic disappearance

was. It was the letter containing my revelation of his secret. The one I had left for my parents in case I disappeared. How was this possible? It was in the pocket of my coat and...

At that point I turned green. As green as goose poo.

"I found it lying on the ground yesterday, after our last lesson. You must have dropped it without realizing. You must forgive me, but I opened the envelope and I read what was in it to find out whom it belonged to."

All of a sudden, I saw his lips transform into a sadistic smile, and he flashed his fangs at me. He looked at me as if I were a big, juicy steak. I heard his tummy rumble. And then they say I have **TOO MUCH** imagination! I was the one eye to eye with a monster!

So I did what I had to do. The only remedy if you're faced with a vampire who is about to bump you off is to flee! I bolted to the door, ran through the corridor and didn't stop until I was outside.

On the street corner I found Julie and Kenza. They were discussing whether to call the police, an ambulance or perhaps the undertaker. I quickly took them with me, away from school. We went to a square where we hid behind some bushes. I told them everything: how the monster had pounced on me without any warning, how he had roared and spread out his cloak, and how his sharp fangs had been a few millimetres from my throat. Then I explained how I had managed to avoid being bitten by hitting him in the teeth with my elbow and running off just as he was transforming himself into a bat...

OK, it's true. Maybe I **EXAGGERATED** just a little bit, but that was because of the shock.

Dear , now you know roughly what happened on the worst day of my life. I feel good about having told you everything, even if the situation is so much more complicated now that Mr *fleder* knows I have discovered his true identity. One thing is for sure, I won't be able to get any sleep tonight. I have barricaded my door and my window, and Roudoudou and I will be keeping watch.

As for school, that's out of the question. I will never set foot in there again!

Friday
17th January

My darling Z,

(I'm **SO** happy!)

Life is full of surprises. And this evening I must have had the **BIGGEST** of them all since my birth! Truly supercalifragilisticexpialidocious (that one I *know* exists, however bizarre it looks)! I'm so excited that I have turned the room on its head by jumping around so much. Poor Roudoudou got so dizzy that he ended up leaving the room, however much of an effort that is for him.

My head is spinning with all the surprises of today. I will try and tell you all that has happened in the correct order to share my JOY with you.

After yesterday's terrible episode in school, I was plagued by nightmares all night. A giant set of teeth held up by a VERY hairy bat followed me in the street with Charmille joking that they wanted to know whether I was afraid of the BAT or the BITE!

I know, it's ridiculous, but you do the best you can with your dreams. As a result I was even more tired when I got up than when I went to bed and I didn't have to resort to play-acting. This morning I was REALLY ill! The electronic thermometer registered 39,5 . I had a headache, and my stomach hurt, as well as my ears, my knees and my left big toe.

I was ill enough to spend the rest of the day in bed. With a bit of luck, I thought, I'd have the rest of the week off too.

I enjoyed having some time away from school. I made the most of my comfy bed, my mum's TLC (she took the day off work for me) and Roudoudou, who spent the morning drooling all over my face, cuddled up against me and purring like mad. When he saw me in such a bad way, he forgave me for all that silly diet business. He's a lovely cat!

So I made the most of the day. Until six o'clock when my dad got home.

I heard his voice. Then my mother's voice. And then a third...

That last voice sounded familiar. TOO familiar. After that, I didn't hear anything any more.

My throat felt really tight. I put Roudoudou down (he protested), I got up (he  miaowed) and I left my room after checking to see if I hadn't left you open on my desk, my dear **Z**. (When I did that, Roudoudou got really angry.) When I got to the corridor, I tried to hear what they were saying. But I couldn't hear a thing. I wanted to call my mother, but my mouth and tongue refused to cooperate. To give myself some courage I picked up a sharp-tipped umbrella that was standing in the corner. If I had to take on the monster, I had better arm myself. Then I tiptoed towards the living room and quietly pushed the door ajar. That is when I saw him, sitting on our sofa. That bloodsucker! He was sitting there relaxed, having a drink with my father and mother...

"Ah, Zazie! There you are!" my mother cried out with a funny kind of smile that gave me the creeps. (What if she had been bitten?)

"I bumped into Mr **Fleder** in front of the school, and since he said he wanted to talk to us, I invited him," my father said.

I stood in the doorway, riveted to the ground. With my eyes I begged my parents to escape through the window. They were having a drink with a **Vampire**! And soon the nibbles would be served: little olives and blobs of blood!

"Don't just stand there! Come and sit with us," my mother said. "And put that umbrella down. It hardly ever rains inside the house…"

I felt my willpower draining away. I dropped my weapon and shuffled towards the sofa, as if hypnotized by the monster.

"Did you bring the letter?" my father asked harshly.

"Mr **fleder** has told us all about your antics in the canteen," my mother added. "You will not be allowed to watch television for a whole week."

It was like being struck by lightning. A whole week! When all I did was hide the letter from my parents to save their lives? SUCH INJUSTICE! Oh well, I am beginning to get used to it...

"Unfortunately, we can't say we're surprised," my mother said turning to Mr **fleder**. "She's the same at home!"

"Sometimes even worse," my father felt he needed to add.

It was my lucky day. Maybe I should have interrupted them to say "Shall we talk about something else?", but I wasn't sure if it was the right moment.

"I think Zazie understands that all that is behind us," Mr **Fleder** said. "But there is something else I wanted to talk to you about."

OH DEAR!

"Oh dear!" my mother exclaimed.

"What have you been up to this time?" my father groaned.

That monster is going to say all sorts of horrendous things about me, I thought.

"I'll show you."

At that moment Mr **Fleder** put his hand in his pocket and took out my red envelope. The one that contains my revelation about his being a _Vampire_.

to be opened in case of tragic disappearance

"What's that?" my father wanted to know.

It was time for me to intervene.

"Something I made up for laughs!"

"There are some bits that can be improved," said Mr **Fleder**, "but it's a good story. Zazie is very imaginative."

"That's putting it mildly," my dad said.

"If you only knew the kinds of things she comes out with!" my mother added.

"She writes very well for a girl her age," Mr **Fleder** said. "You ought to encourage her to continue writing."

I looked at my teacher, dumbstruck. My jaws dropped. Instead of pouncing on us to devour us, this **Vampire** was complimenting me on my writing? Was that a clever trick or what?

"I can't say I'm surprised," my father said, sinking into his armchair with pride. "My wife and I passed on the reading bug. I even need to keep an eye out on what she reads. The other day she wanted to read **DRACULA**! I told her she was too young for that."

At that point Mr **Fleder** turned to me and did something **INCREDIBLE**. He smiled at me! He gave me a real smile! However hard I looked into his eyes, I couldn't detect any cruelty. On the contrary, he looked perfectly kind-hearted.

REAL SMILE

"Books are great, **ZAZIE**. But you have to be careful not to confuse reality and fiction, you know?"

Everything started to swim. It was as if I were looking at the living room from within a fishbowl: everything was muffled and deformed. Mr **Fleder** gave

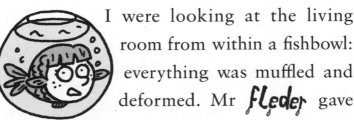

157

me my envelope back. I accepted it without saying a word, my mouth still wide open (I must hold the world record of looking stupid!).

"Continue writing," my teacher encouraged me. "You're talented."

I looked at Mr **Fleder**. I was flabbergasted. I had the impression something in his face had changed. His eyes looked more kindly, his eyebrows were less bushy and his canine teeth seemed shorter... Had I been completely wrong about him? Yes, I had been under the spell of **DRACULA** – not an actual vampire, but... the book!

Mr **Fleder** got up, saying he had to be off. My parents thanked him. I remained rooted to my chair. Mr **Fleder** waved at me before he left.

My parents turned to me. My dad looked at the envelope and said: "Well, Zazie? Are you going to read your story to us?"

For the first time in a long while, my parents actually listened to what I had to say and paid close attention. They smiled, looked in horror and rolled their eyes as they were listening to my incredible story. And when it was finished, to my big surprise, they applauded…

How wrong you can be about people sometimes. In fact, it turns out my parents are actually really quite nice!

When I walked back to my room, clasping the envelope to my breast, I felt light-headed. Ever since that moment I've only had one all-consuming wish: *To write stories*   .

Saturday
25th January

My dearest Z,

(Who is going to have to forgive his dear *darling Zazie* – please?)

I'm sorry, my beloved Z, that I haven't written on your pretty white pages for more than a week. But I have a good excuse. I started writing a thrilling story in a big exercise book my parents gave me (no need to be jealous, it's not as pretty as you), and it has taken up a lot of my time (don't look so cross, I haven't even given it a name).

So what's the story about? I haven't told anyone, but you know how to keep a secret, don't you? It is the story of a young girl and her fat cat called Karateka, who need to protect their family against a horrible pair of twin witches called Charmille! It's a story full of twists and turns and awesome descriptions. Sounds good, right?

Now for today's great news: Mrs Cuche is coming back to school! At last we'll be able to relax and chat and have a good time... To have our lives back, if you know what I mean! After a month of Mr **Fleder** and his hellish work schedule we need a break.

We still don't know why Mrs Cuche was absent. This morning Anaïs swore it was because she had been on maternity leave after giving birth to triplets. At sixty! I was obliged to tell her (for her own sake) that she always talks RUBBISH. After that, we argued and fell out (as always).

Julie and Kenza asked me why I had stopped trying to catch the *Vampire*. I took on my most mysterious air and told them I had made a pact with Mr *Fleder* after finding his weakness, thanks to the novel *DRACULA*. I would allow him to escape with his life as long as he would leave us pupils alone.

The girls were VERY impressed, except Anaïs, who was spying on us and told me that I always talked such RUBBISH (no comment).

All the same, it will be hard to forget Mr *Fleder*. He was VERY scary and made us work like slaves, but thanks to his

163

encouragement I will soon be *THE MOST FAMOUS* of all writers in ~~my borough the city the country~~ the whole world!

Thanks to his encouragement... and also thanks to you, my dear ⚡! It was your pretty white pages that made me want to write in the first place.

If Auntie Bea hadn't put you under the Christmas tree, everything would have been different... That means it turned out the way it did because of Auntie Bea. Or rather, because of granny and granddad, the parents of Auntie Bea and my dad. Because without them, Auntie Bea and my dad would not have been born, and as a result I wouldn't be here either.

But granny and granddad also have parents... Jeez Louise ! I'd better stop myself here.

My brain is bubbling again. I just can't help it! There are always so many ideas whirling around in my head!

What can I say? That's what *imagination* is: both a blessing and a curse.

Sunday
26th January

Z! Z! Z!

(It's very urgent!)

Sorry to disturb you after 10 p.m., but you are the only one who can comfort me after what I've seen this evening. The horror has started again!!!

At the beginning of this evening I started *The War of the Worlds*, a novel by H.G. Wells. It's about the invasion of Earth by bad-tempered extraterrestrials who destroy everything in their path.

Why are they so mean? Because these aliens are **VERY** ugly and they live on a hideous planet. They are jealous and want to avenge themselves on our beautiful Earth and human beings like myself (that is to say, on all the *beautiful* people).

I was quietly reading about how their extra-terrestrial laser beams can cut a house in two, really enjoying myself and imagining that house was Anaïs's, when a strange, metallic and piercing noise spoilt it for me. I thought at first it was Roudoudou's miaowing, but it wasn't... It came from outside.

When I turned my head to the window, I saw a strange blue light illuminating my room. I grabbed my cuddly penguin, who was **VERY**

scared, got out of bed and walked over to the window…

You'll never guess what happened! The blue light came from Mrs Farigoule's house, our hideous and repulsive neighbour! She's an old hag who spends her time barking at the kids in our neighbourhood, like a badly trained bulldog. She gets wound up about the tiniest things.

I cut three pathetic little flowers from her garden to give to my mum on Mother's Day and she explodes like a volcano. I paint a pretty little pumpkin on her letterbox for Halloween, and she threatens to give me a hiding! In short, she's pure evil.

I immediately felt something terrible was going on when I heard that piercing noise and saw the blue light coming out of her house. I looked at her bay window and saw shadows appearing, doing a funny kind of dance.

A blue light, strange shadows, odd noises in the middle of the night… Are you thinking what I'm thinking?

There's no doubt about it: Mrs Farigoule is an extraterrestrial scout who has come to prepare the Earth for the invasion. That seems to me to be the only ⇒ LOGICAL CONCLUSION. And that explains why she's so ugly, with her big greenish head that scares even Roudoudou, her legs covered in scabs that look like the scales of a snake and her flowery aprons that hurt your eyes when you even look at them. Her ugliness is *out of this world!*

BiG GREENISH HEAD

HORRIBLE APRON

SNAKE-SCALE SCABS

I immediately went to my parents in the living room to tell them about my terrible discovery. As they had fallen asleep in front of the telly, I had to shake them a bit to wake them up. They were not in the best of moods. True, maybe I had shouted a little too loudly in Mum's ear. And true, maybe I jumped on Dad's belly a bit too vigorously, but if you believe it's so easy to wake up grownups... In the end they sighed in exasperation, refused to listen to a word I had to say and sent me straight back to bed.

SLURP

Too bad for them. At least I warned them. If they come crying to me later when one of the aliens has gobbled up their brain, they can't expect me to feel sorry for them!

If that's how things stand, I'll face them alone. From tomorrow onwards, I will put a plan together to unmask . It's between you and me now, Mrs Farigoule from outer space!

As for you, my dear darling , don't worry. Nothing can happen to you. As long as {ZAZIE} watches over you, no one will bother you. No one.

Oh no… Roudoudou!!!

Many thanks to Talie for reading this,
giving me advice, sharing her ideas and
helping {**ZAZIE**} grow up.

Jean-Marcel Erre was born in the south of France in 1971, and works as a teacher in Montpellier. He also writes novels, TV sketches and screenplays.